This igloo book belongs to:

....

Contents

Amy's Game .... page 4

Fiona's Post .... page 12

Billy and Cuddles .... page 20

The Lost Yellow Ball .... page 28

Tomboy Tina .... page 36

Bedtime for Ted .... page 44

igloobooks

Published in 2019
by Igloo Books Ltd
Cottage Farm
Sywell
NN6 0BJ
www.igloobooks.com

Copyright © 2011 Igloo Books Ltd
Igloo Books is an imprint of Bonnier Books UK

1019 001
2 4 6 8 10 9 7 5 3 1
ISBN 978-1-78810-570-5

Illustrated by Mike Garton
Written by Melanie Joyce

Printed and manufactured in China

Stories for

Year Olds

igloobooks

Amy's Game

Daddy said to Amy, "Let's play hide-and-seek. I'll count from one to ten. I promise I won't peek. 1-2-3-4-5-6-7-8-9-10."

Then, Dad crept across the carpet. He looked behind the door. He peered into the closet and all around the floor. "Where are you, Amy?" he asked.

Dad opened up the lid of Amy's green toy box.
Then, he looked inside the jumper drawer and the
drawer stuffed full of socks.

"Where could she be?" said Dad. Then he looked under the bed. "Amy isn't here, either," and then he scratched his head.

He went into the hallway and peered right down the stairs. "Amy's good at hiding," said Dad. "I can't find her anywhere."

Then, someone gave a chuckle. They shuffled and they wriggled. From underneath the pink bedspread, there came a little giggle.

So, Dad crept across the carpet. He peeped and then said, "BOO!"
Amy jumped up squealing and Dad said, "I found you!"

"It's my turn to hide," said Dad. "Remember now, don't peek."
So, Amy counted from one to ten. She loved playing hide-and-seek.

Fiona's Post

Fiona didn't like it when the postman came to call. He lurked behind the letterbox and dropped letters in the hall.

He made the garden gate go creak and shut it with a *thwack*. Then, he crunched along the gravel path, carrying his letter sack.

One very special morning, the delivery was late.
Then, suddenly, Fiona heard the creaking of the gate.

14

The postman rang the bell and Fiona ran to hide.
She crept under the stairs, in case Mum let him inside.

Fiona peeped out at the postman. He was big and very tall. He handed Mum a parcel and she put it by the wall.

16

The postman said the parcel had come from far away. "It's for you, Fiona," he said, "because today is your birthday."

In the parcel was a lovely teddy, from Fiona's Auntie Sue. The postman delivered it especially and Fiona said, "Thank you."

18

Fiona was very glad the postman had
come to call. She waved and gave him a
great big smile – he wasn't frightening at all.

Billy and Cuddles

Billy and Cuddles loved the rain. They watched it drip-drop down the window pane.
"Can we go outside and splash about?" Billy asked.

"Yes," said Mum, "but both of you must put on your wellies and your raincoats. Remember now, don't get too muddy or wet."

21

Outside, Cuddles saw a puddle and she jumped in the middle. The water splashed Billy and it made Cuddles giggle.

So, Billy gave a jump and sploshed in a puddle.
It was very muddy and splattered Cuddles.
"My turn," said Cuddles, with a chuckle and she
looked for another muddy puddle.

But the puddle was deep and the water began to creep down Cuddles' boots and between her toes. "It's cold!" she cried.

24

Cuddles jiggled her boots, this way and that.
But she jiggled too much and whoops, she slipped
into the very muddy puddle.

"I'm wet," said Billy, "and so are you Cuddles.
I think I've had enough of jumping in puddles."
So, they went back home to play inside.

26

Mum gave them cupcakes and fizzy lemonade.
"We still love the rain," said Billy and Cuddles,
"especially jumping in puddles."

The Lost Yellow Ball

Ned and Lola had lost their big yellow ball.
So, they sniffed all over the house. Then they sniffed
in the garden.

There was something round on the ground, in the vegetable patch. "It's our ball!" said Ned. But when he sniffed it, "Pooh!" he cried. "It's just a smelly old cabbage."

"I'll look in the shed," said Lola and she sniffed and sniffed. But the shed was dark and full of spiders hanging in cobwebs.

30

Sniff, sniff went Lola. But a big spider ran onto her nose. "Urgh!" she cried, jumping and bumping into Dad's garden tools, that clanged and clattered with a terrible noise.

Lola bounded out of the shed and across the lawn. Then, with one big leap, she jumped over the wall. There was something squashy and soft on the other side.

"It's our big yellow ball," said Ned. "Well done, Lola, you found it after all."

All afternoon, Ned and Lola had fun with their ball.
It went *boing* on the shed and *bounce-bounce* on
the wall.

34

They ran around and giggled, then ran around some more. Ned and Lola were happy. They loved their big yellow ball.

Tomboy Tina

Tina's mum was having a party. "Cousin Zara is coming early to play," she said. "Do you want to put on a dress and some shoes?"

But Tina just shook her head. "I don't want a dress or shoes," she said. "I want to wear my scruffy dungarees, so I can climb up trees."

But then, Cousin Zara arrived. She sparkled like stars, all glitter and spangles. She wore a fancy hairband and red jingly bangles.

Zara twirled on her tiptoes and it seemed to Tina that she was just like a fairy, or a ballerina.

Tina thought Zara was terribly clever. "I want to be just like you," she said. "You're the best cousin, ever."

"Shall I show you how?" asked Zara. "You don't have to wear shoes or a dress." That made Tina smile. She nodded and said, "Yes!"

Zara helped Tina to pick out some clothes.
She gave her bracelets and hairbands and put
pink polish on her toes.

Soon, Tina was ready for the party. Mum gave her a squeeze. "You look beautiful, Tina," she said, "even in dungarees."

Bedtime for Ted

It was night-time in Edward's house. But he wouldn't go to bed. "I'm not going," he said to Dad, "not without Big Ted."

Dad and Edward looked high and low and searched from here to there. But they simply couldn't spot Big Ted hiding anywhere.

Then, Dad said, "Look, I can see a furry head.
I've found your teddy, Edward – he's already in the bed."

"Naughty Big Ted," said Edward, but he gave him a cuddle. Because at bedtime there's nothing like a teddy to snuggle.

"Goodnight, Edward," said Dad. "Goodnight, Teddy."
But there was no reply because they were asleep already.